HE NEVER SAYS GOODBYE TO ANYONE

JOSHUA SEY

Joshua Sey

TABLE OF CONTENTS

Joshua Sey

INTRODUCTION

This is an interesting short Novel packed with shear resilience and hardwork on the side of the subject who happens to be a female by the name Ampomah.

In this Novel, you will not just find it interesting but you will learn new things like patience and commitment towards anything you do in life.

He Never Says Goodbye To Anyone

CHAPTER ONE

It was a very bright morning.

The early morning sun has risen, and all the athletes were ready to leave the training pitch for their homes; they needed to rest their spines after a tiring training session.

The athletes had been chosen from across the nation. They were the best among the nations numerous athletes, and having chalked so much success in local athletic competitions, they were to represent the nation in the oncoming Olympic Games in Dubai.

Seeing the big task ahead of them, the athletes worked harder and were well prepared to win honors for themselves and make the nation proud.

The female athletes had just showered down, packed up their training kits and were heading for their bus, outside the training pitch, when out of the blue Ampöma began to behave abnormally; she shouted indiscriminately, rolled on the ground and hopped around like a fleeing toad

He Never Says Goodbye To Anyone

"You must be kidding." She yelled with a pointed finger that aimed at no one in particular, "You can't participate in the Olympics. No, not whilst I'm alive."

At first, Ampoman's strange behaviour was taken lightly by her observers. Such jokes were common among athletes. But now they wondered why it should be Ampomah of all people.

That is unlike the real her. Something must have prompted this unusual attitude in an extremely quiet and habitually shy Ampomah.

What an eyesore! She had begun to dance and strip herself naked, not even minding the presence of the opposite sex. Is she mimicking strip dancers? That is an absolute awkward behaviour, and all her female contemporaries were deeply embarrassed. She was virtually naked and that was more or less shaming the female race.

"Dress up, Ampomah the guys are here." One of the girls hinted her in a whisper. But Ampomah was neither listening nor was she going to stop. Now she was completely naked. Some of the shameless boys giggled at the sight of her nakedness. Just then Mr. Bagoe, the instructor appeared.

"Stop that awful behaviour, you." Shouted Mr. Bagoe, with a thunderous voice, and all at once the girls hurried themselves into their buses. They were sorry for the girl she had been caught and was likely to be expelled from the team.

They had all these while been wishing that the instructor should not come to the scene to perceive Ampomah's mischievous act. But now not only had he seen it all, but he was busy trying to bring Ampomah to order.

He Never Says Goodbye To Anyone

"Would you do as I have said?" the grim faced instructor ordered, "pick up your clothing and behave yourself." But Ampomah was neither dressing up nor was she going to behave herself. She had rather selected stones and was giggling to herself as she glared at the stones.

Mr. Bagoe was really irritated by her nonchalance. But then, it suddenly occurred to him that the girl could be suffering from some form of mental derailment, and no sooner had he come to this realization than the girl began to throw stones at him.

She was armed with stones and too aggressive to be disarmed by the instructor alone. So Mr. Bagoe fled into the bus for cover, and then called up the security guards who encircled Ampomah, disarmed her and bundled her in a cab. Whilst she was being taken to the asylum for medical attention, the other girls looked on with much pity for Ampomah.

A few minutes later it was confirmed by the senior psychiatric officer that Ampomah was having a severe mental problem.

"She would have to be hospitalized and given serious medical attention," Dr. Bedu suggested, "she is suffering from a serious brain damage." Thus, Ampomah was admitted in the mental asylum and bind to prevent her from causing any havoc.

When the news of Ampomah's insanity got to her mother, Mame Serwa broke down and cried bitterly.

He Never Says Goodbye To Anyone

CHAPTER TWO
"Oh my daughter." She wept,

"Who did this to you? And why has life been so unfair to us ever after the death of your father?"

Mame Serwa had been an unhappy woman ever since she lost her husband Mr. Brobbey to a fatal motor accident. She had been struck by a series of mis fortune since then; first it was herself, she had contracted strange swellings all over her body and was physically deformed by the illness.

Next, it was her older daughter Beyinwa; she had woken up one morning feeling a severe headache and running a temperature. She was rushed to the hospital where she was declared dead a short while afterwards.

He Never Says Goodbye To Anyone

Beyinwa was then divorced and every accusing finger pointed to her ex-husband with whom she had a two year old daughter. Benyiwa and her husband had been a happy couple before the man lost his job.

Even then Benyiwa tried to sustain him and not let his joblessness get the best of him. But contrary to her desire, her husband sought solace in alcoholic beverages. In no time, he had become an addicted drunk.

He left home in the late mornings when he had consumed his best breakfast, which his wife had prepared him before going to her work place and returned late in the night heavily drunk.

Benyiwa tried to talk him into changing his way but he worsened each day. The worse of it all was his hostility; he pounced on his wife and beat her severely every often and when she couldn't bare it anymore she divorced him.

Benyiwa had since then moved to her mother's place and lived happily with her mother, her younger sister and her daughter, Serwa, until her untimely death.

As if all these lost were not enough, Mame Serwa was losing yet another daughter to lunacy.

"What have I done wrong?" Mame Serwa sobbed bitterly as tears streaked down her cheeks. "Whom have I offended? Oh Ampomah my only daughter. You are my last hope. Your sudden nomination as a member of the Olympic team gave me a lot of hopes. But now what do I hear? Why am I losing everything I have worked tirelessly to achieve?"

By now little Serwa who was named after her maternal grandmother knew something was wrong. She is four years old now and understood a few things. She knew that Aunt Serwa was in danger and she was very sad, too.

He Never Says Goodbye To Anyone

"Will Aunt Serwa die?" She asked her grand mother, tearfully, whilst wiping out the grandmothers tears with a handkerchief. "I don't want her to die. She is my only aunt. I love her so much."

"Aunt Serwa would not die." The grandmother replied, "But we must pray for her. She is seriously sick. We need to pray for God's intervention, Serwa"

Meanwhile the Minister of Sports had personally hired a special physiatrist from China to cure Ampoma of her mental illness.

He did not want such a great potential to go down the drain; she had performed too exceptionally well and impressed many fans to be omitted from the Olympic team. That was obviously a great loss to the sports ministry and the nation at large.

Many sports analysts had tipped her to be the most promising athlete among her contemporaries and they were optimistic that the nation was losing a great athlete to lunacy. Thus, the minister's action was applauded by all well meaning Ghanaians and sports lovers.

Tried as the minister and many influential citizens of the country did to help Ampoma out of her illness, her situation deteriorated. She had turned very aggressive and has attacked many staff's of the hospital. Owing to the severity of her illness she was kept in a special cage, to prevent her from hurting others.

Many of Mame Serwa's relatives and well wishers came to express their sympathy. Among such sympathizers was Mama Ejafua. She had come all the way from Sunasi, in the Eastern Region to share in the misery of her cousin, Mame Serwa. Mame Serwa was very grateful that her cousin had come.

He Never Says Goodbye To Anyone

CHAPTER THREE

The two ladies had spent their childhood and teenage together in Sunasi, sharing many glorious moments together and being the best of friends. As beautiful young ladies back then, it was their ardent desire to get married to the richest men in the society and have a happy family.

Their dreams was partly achieved when they both got married to the men of affluence, in the same wedding ceremony, in the same church auditorium and united by the same priest on the same day of the same year.

Almost four decades down the line, the story had changed and both ladies were grieving rather than rejoicing, Mame Ejafua was the first to be struck by tragedy. She had been barren for two decades in her marriage to Major General Twum.

He Never Says Goodbye To Anyone

Her military husband blamed her bareness on her and took a mistress, who bore him two sons and a daughter. Then, her husband fled home and was glued to his mistress and her children.

He however came back home to her when his mistress and her children got burnt down in their apartment one fateful night, whilst the General was on a mission to the Middle-East.

The General left home without trace afterwards, having consistently complained about Mame Ejafua's bareness and did not return home ever after.

It was as though the ladies were partners in misery; for, no sooner had Mame Ejafua's husband fled without trace than Mame Serwa also lost her husband to alcohol. This was followed by the ruin of her skin, and subsequently the death of her daughter and eventually Ampomah's dilemma. Throughout all these troubles Mama Ejafua had been solidly behind her cousin.

"We shall triumph over our enemies. My sister Mame Ejafua comforted her cousin, "This is definitely not our portion in life we weren't born losers. God will in his own time restore all our loss and we shall laugh aloud and shame our enemies. So take heart and let's hold on to our faith in God."

Several visits to the psychiatric hospital revealed that Ampomah would hardly recover from her illness. This report was a great source of sorrow to Mame Serwa. But her cousin wouldn't allow her to despair. Most especially when she knew there was a way out.

"I have consistently told you not to throw in the towel so soon, sister," she said trying to re-assure her cousin, who was all tears, "I know a powerful herbalist in a remote village near our hometown that can cure her of this illness.

He Never Says Goodbye To Anyone

"This kind of disease can not be cured by orthodox medicine, you know. We must take her to the herbalist. He has a camp where he treats all forms of mental disability I bet she would be okay once she got there."

So saying, Ampomah was conveyed to a psychiatric home, situated in a deserted village where an old herbalist attended to numerous mentally derailed patients.

Ampomah spent some more days in the psychiatric home yet her situation remained unchanged. Although, she had calmed down a bit, she was now more or less an imbecile. Filled with doubts about her daughter's soundness, Mame Serwa asked the herbalist why Ampomah had suddenly become timid and inactive.

"Nana," she said respectfully, "Why is she looking rather timid now?"

"That's the beginning of her recovery." The old herbalist cut in reassuringly, "She is calming down now. That is good for her. It means that she is responding to the treatment being given her and I hope that she would soon be completely cured of her illness."

With this assurance Mame Serwa went home, having paid a huge sum of money to the herbalist as Ampomah's treatment fee. Although her unsightly looks had prevented her from doing any social trade, the passionate minister of sports was always at her aid, asking to be updated about the girl's health and giving her mother the necessary financial backing.

"It's just about a fortnight to the Olympic Games," the minister informed Mame Serwa, "do you think Ampomah can make it to the game? I don't want her to miss out."

"The herbalist said she will recover soon, sir." Mame Serwa replied, "But I don't know how soon.

He Never Says Goodbye To Anyone

CHAPTER FOUR

"I just hope that she recovers and join her mates. The minister said, "Everybody wants to see her back.

"I hope so too." Replied Mame Serwa.

"So do I," added little Serwa, who was very passionate about her aunt's revival,

The minister was touched by the little girl's concern though her grandmother was embarrassed by her interruption in an elderly discussion.

"You know what?" the minister said turning to Mame Serwa, "My bible tells me that Jesus loves little children. If you can go on your knees and pray for your aunt, God will answer your prayers and heal her."

He Never Says Goodbye To Anyone

No sooner as the minister left Mame Serwa's home, than little Serwas began to pray for her aunt, Ampomah.

"Lord Jesus," she began, "I know you are the greatest healer. I also learnt that you love little children like me. Please have mercy on my aunt, Serwa. You know she loves me so much.

"She always did her best to make me happy and had taught me a lot of good things.

Please cure her of her sickness and let her come back home to us. Thank you Lord for an answered prayer, amen."

Just then Benyiwa's apparition appeared to Ampomah and spoke to her.

"Ampomah my sister." She echoed. Only Ampomah heard and saw her, "Our enemies have chosen to make our mother grieve all her life. But little did they know that their ways are not God's ways. Today you will be liberated from the clutches of the devil. You are freed."

At that moment, the chains with which Ampomah was bound broke loose.

"Do not go back home." The apparition ordered, "Go to the sports minister and you shall be received heartily by your contemporaries and thrive in your carear. It's your time to shine and put our enemies to shame. Take good care of your niece and show much love to mother. They had been praying fervently for you."

The apparition disappeared and then Ampomah realized that she bad been insane. She looked around and saw all sorts of sick people. She examined herself and realized that she was in rags. It can't be me. She told herself.

He Never Says Goodbye To Anyone

"Go!" the voice of her sister's apparition echoed again. And all at once she threw her shackle away and raced off. The herbalist was just on time. He came to the yard just as Ampomah was dashing out through the gates of the yard.

He was mystified at the sight. Where is her shackle? He found it lying on the ground. How did she unbind herself? Did someone rescue her? He looked around for an outsider and saw no one. She mightn't have rescued herself. No. she has no such power.

The herbalist immediately called out to his assistants, "Gado, Babu, Santo and Hakilu!"

"Yes Nana!" the herbalist's assistants replied and appeared almost immediately. The men could sense trouble. For the herbalist's tone was hasher than normal. And the urgency with which he invited them said it all.

"That mad girl, Ampomah has raced off." The herbalist informed the men, pointing at the direction of the wooden gate. "Go after her now and bring her to me." The men were already racing after Ampomah even before the herbalist finished his statement.

Ampomah gave the men a good run for their money. But just as she was about to negotiate the only curve that led to the village, the men draw level with her and made to capture her. Out of total despair Ampomah screamed, "Help!" and all at once her sister's apparition appeared.

A blazing flame accompanied Benyiwa's arrival and made a boundary between Ampomah and the men preventing them from drawing any closer to her. Shivers immediately ran down the men's spine as a coarse voice emerged from the flame and warned them to retreat lest the worse occurs to them.

He Never Says Goodbye To Anyone

CHAPTER FIVE

"Depart from her!" the raging voice cautioned, "Depart lest I vent my vengeful wrath on you." The fretful men fled as fast as they could, not even turning or tossing their heads. Ampomah was really baffled at how the men had instantly retreated.

A moment ago she had thought that she was going back into captivity but all of a sudden her captives had withdrawn from arresting her and she couldn't understand why they had suddenly decided to let go of her.

She mustn't spend the next thirty minutes in this village she must be on her way to the city before hand. She looked around and saw virtually everyone starring at her. Their eyes were sternly fixed on her and all at once she read their thoughts. She must do something to clear the mist and also to win favour of these people.

He Never Says Goodbye To Anyone

So she went on her knees and pleaded, "Please help me, good people. I am not mad as you think. I am a profession athlete. I was in training camp, preparing for the Olympic Games when my adversaries cast a spell on me. They brought me to the camp just to let everyone forget about me.

"Please help me. I must be in the city within the shortest possible time. I am helpless and desperately in need of you assistance. Remember the scripture says that there is much blessing in giving. Please help!"

Struck by her sermon the people of Botukora walked up to Ampomah and slipped both notes and coins generously into her palm, and wished her good luck in her future endeavour. She was made to bathe, after which she was given a blouse, a wrapper and a scarf to cover the dreadlocks she had derived from many days of insanity.

Joshua Sey

I must be in the city within the shortest possible time.

He Never Says Goodbye To Anyone

Her team mates had just begun the days training session, that bright Saturday morning, when Ampoma appeared in the company of the sports minister.

"Hello everybody your home girl is back!" she hailed out to her colleagues and without any much ado all her friends had gathered around her. They lifted her shoulder high and chanted slogans jubilantly.

Two weeks later Ampomah was in Dubai with the team. Geared up by her past experience, she performed incredibly beyond everybody's expectation and won many gold medals in her field of athleticism. She also won many monetary prizes and was invited to several international athletic competitions.

When she arrived home, she was hailed as a heroine. She got a brand new Pajero, a flat and a lot of money for her hard work. A Street was as well named after her. Her mother couldn't hide her joy when her daughter drove her in her Pajero car and ushered her into her new apartment.

Joshua Sey

He Never Says Goodbye To Anyone

He Never Says Goodbye To Anyone

Joshua Sey

He Never Says Goodbye To Anyone

Joshua Sey

He Never Says Goodbye To Anyone

Joshua Sey

He Never Says Goodbye To Anyone

He Never Says Goodbye To Anyone

Joshua Sey

He Never Says Goodbye To Anyone

He Never Says Goodbye To Anyone

Joshua Sey

He Never Says Goodbye To Anyone

Joshua Sey

He Never Says Goodbye To Anyone

Joshua Sey

He Never Says Goodbye To Anyone

He Never Says Goodbye To Anyone

He Never Says Goodbye To Anyone

Joshua Sey

He Never Says Goodbye To Anyone

Joshua Sey

He Never Says Goodbye To Anyone

Joshua Sey

He Never Says Goodbye To Anyone

Joshua Sey

He Never Says Goodbye To Anyone

Joshua Sey

He Never Says Goodbye To Anyone

He Never Says Goodbye To Anyone

He Never Says Goodbye To Anyone

Joshua Sey

He Never Says Goodbye To Anyone

Joshua Sey

He Never Says Goodbye To Anyone

Joshua Sey

He Never Says Goodbye To Anyone

Joshua Sey

He Never Says Goodbye To Anyone

Joshua Sey

He Never Says Goodbye To Anyone

CHAPTER SIX

Two weeks later, just as Ampomah was about to embark on a journey to France, to participate in an athletic competition, Ampomah heard a news that she could hardly believe; her mother's cousin, Mame Ejafua was said to have confessed to certain atrocious deeds;

She was said to have admitted being behind all the tragedy that had befallen Mame Serwa and her family she had sought the assistance of a voodoo priest to make Mr. Brobbey lost his job, cast a spell on Mame Serwa, kill Beyinwa and also to make Ampoma run mad.

She did all these because she was jealous of her cousin who seems to have all her heart's desire a loving husband, a happy family and lovely children. All these she had lacked ever since she got married to her military husband.

She couldn't stand seeing her cousin and childhood friend being better of than she was. So she resorted to evil. But God was on the side of the innocent. Her own evil deeds haunted her and now she was confessing her evil and asking for pardon.

The End.